The
Empty
Space

Marianna Sztyma

The Empty Space

London 2017

centrala
every book matters

First published in Great Britain 2017 by Centrala Ltd.
27B Khama Road
London SW17 0EN
www.centrala.org.uk

Copyright © Centrala Ltd. / Marianna Sztyma
Translation copyright David Malcolm
Proofread by Sean Gasper Bye
Editorial & Publishing Director: Michał Słomka
DTP: gabinet.co.uk

Printed and bound in Poland

ISBN 978-1-912278-00-8

Order from www.centrala.org.uk

I gather up your tears.
Sometimes you cry
when you think of her.

Come on then. We'll cry together. I've got a whole supply of your tears.

Why?
Because my kitty was tiny and you're big. You should be as tiny as she was. Then I'd cuddle you.

CENTRALA BOOKS

Forest Beekeeper and Treasure of Pushcha by Tomasz Samojlik
Blacky. Four of Us by Mateusz Skutnik
Adventures on a Desret Island by Maciej Sieńczyk
Fertility by Mikołaj Pasiński & Gosia Herba
Dear Rikard by Lene Ask
Tuff Ladies by Till Lukat
Moscow by Øystein Runde & Ida Neverdahl
Friends by Jan Soeken
Locomotive/IDEOLO by Małgorzata Gurowska, Joanna Ruszczyk & Julian Tuwim
Comics Cookbook by V/A
Do You Miss Your Country? by Monika Szydłowska
Chernobyl. The Zone by Natacha Bustos & Francisco Sánchez
Erik the Red – King of Winter by Søren Mosdal
Elephant on the Moon by Mikołaj Pasiński & Gosia Herba
Disco Cry by Marianna Serocka
Anubis by Joanna Karpowicz
Hungry Hansel and Gluttonous Gretel by Zavka
Old Farts by Sorina Vazelina

www.centrala.org.uk